NICK®

SpongeBob SquarePants

You Can't Keep a Good Sponge Down

by David Lewman

POCKET BOOKS
New York London Toronto Sydney Bikini Bottom

POCKET BOOKS, a division of Simon & Schuster, Inc.
1230 Avenue of the Americas, New York, NY 10020

First published in Great Britain in 2004 by Simon & Schuster UK Ltd

ISBN:1-4165-0048-0

First Pocket Books trade paperback edition November 2004

10 9 8 7 6 5 4 3 2 1

POCKET and colophon are registered trademarks of Simon & Schuster, Inc.

Manufactured in the United States of America

For information regarding special discounts for bulk purchases, please contact
Simon & Schuster Special Sales at 1-800-456-6798 or business@simonandschuster.com

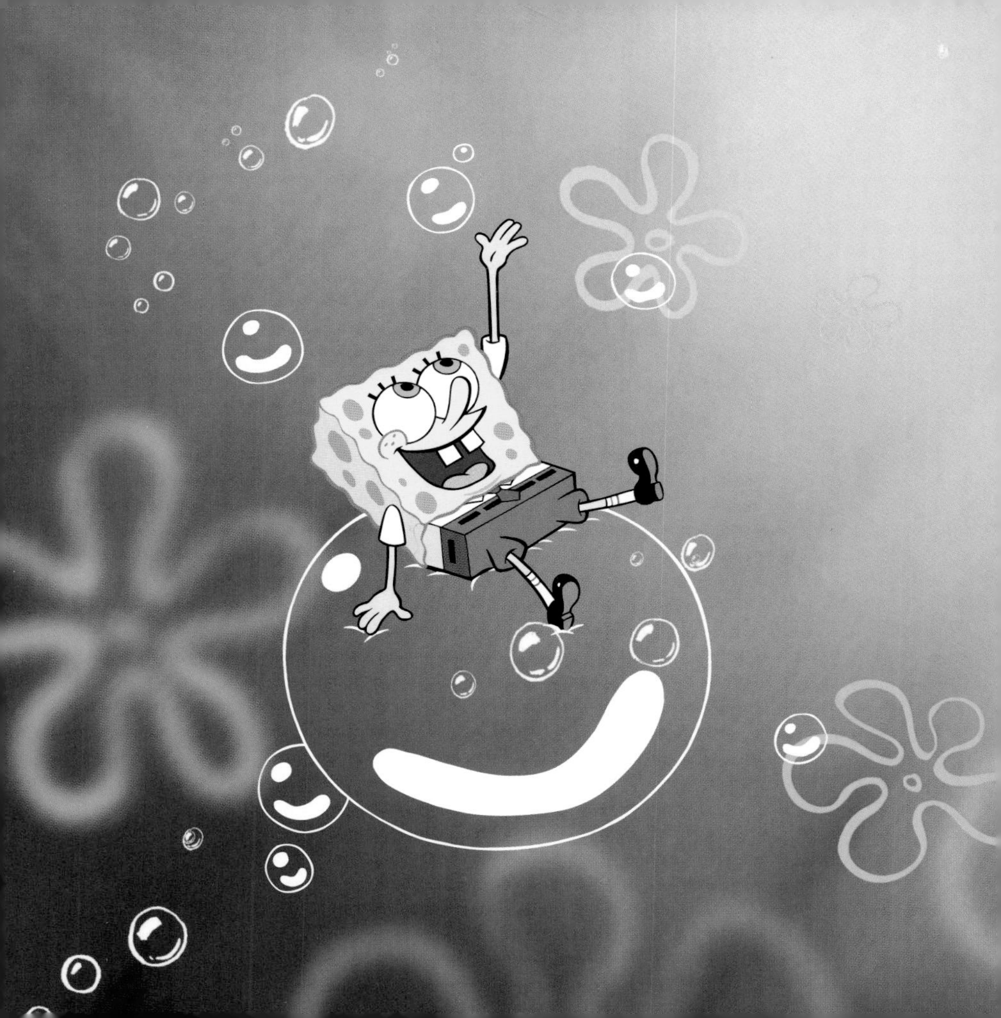

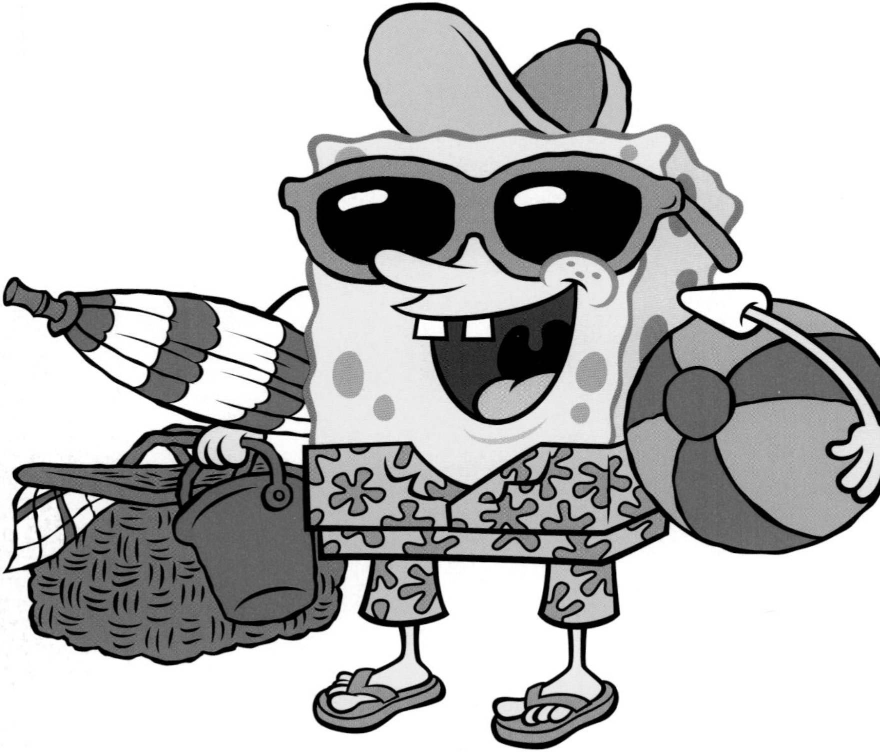

SpongeBob is an expert on happiness.

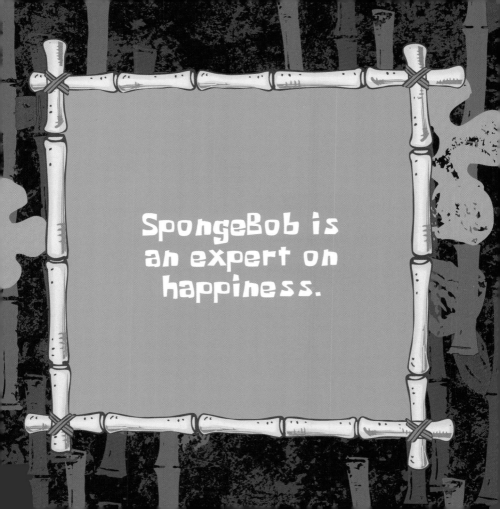

i am a HAPPY
sponge!

8

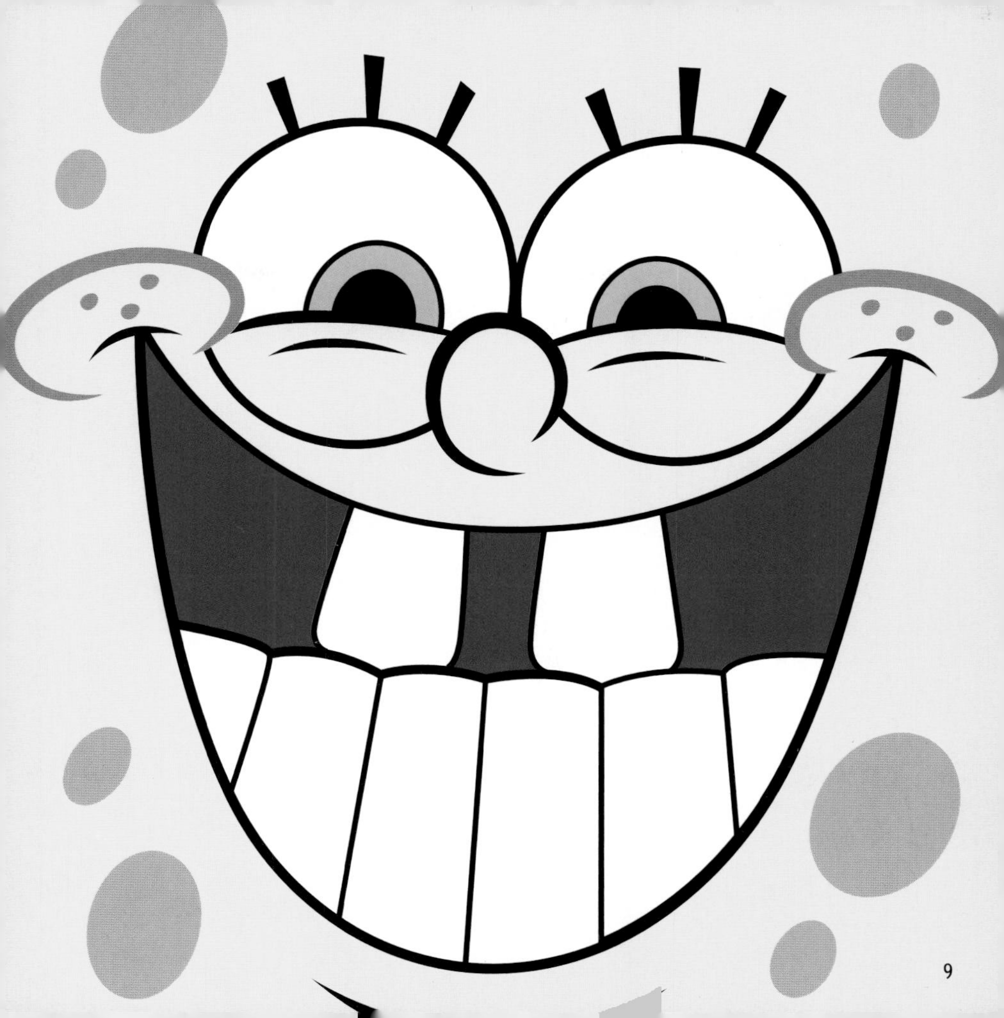

And he's willing
to share his secrets.

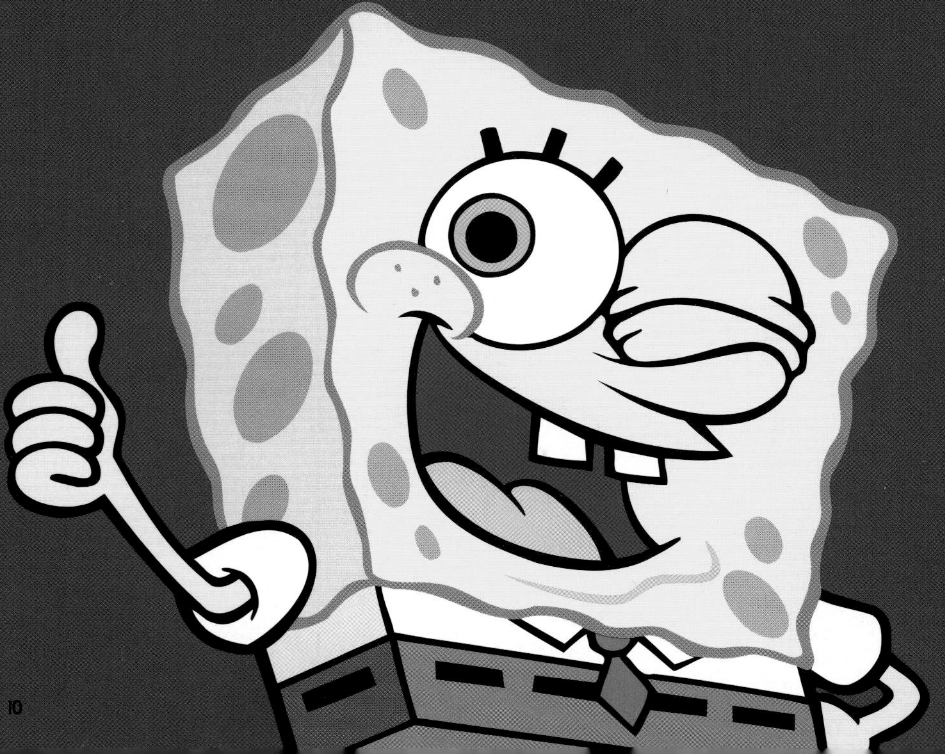

it's no secret that the best thing about a secret is secretly telling someone your secret. Thereby secretly adding another secret to their secret collection of secrets... secretly.

Here are some of SpongeBob's best secrets.

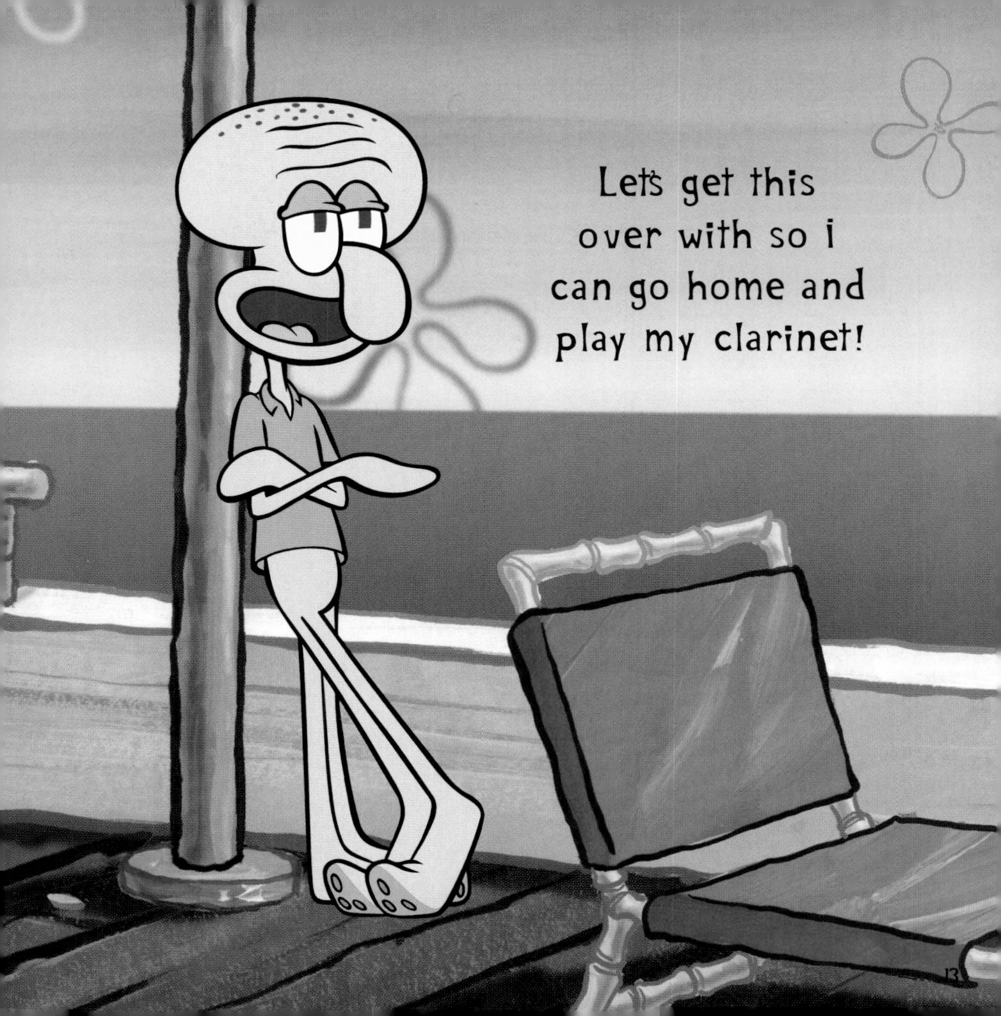
Let's get this over with so i can go home and play my clarinet!

Having

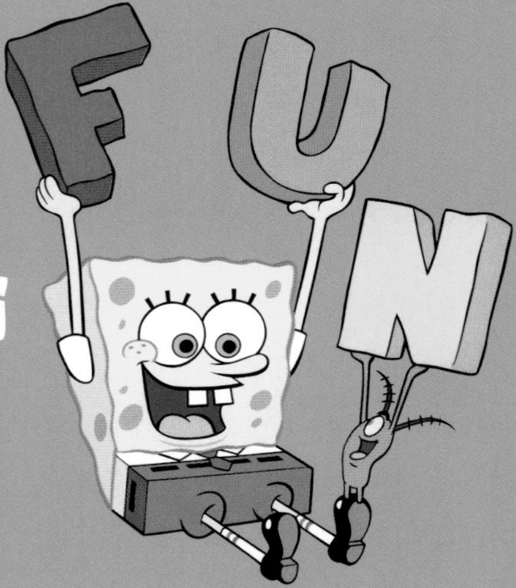
FUN

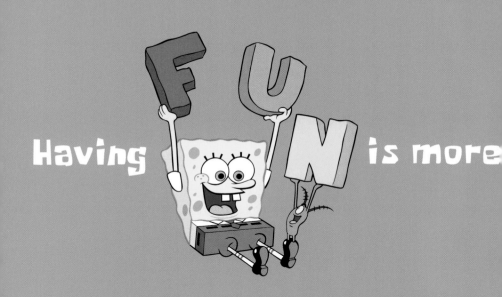

is more

i Feel all TiNGLY inside. Should we stop?

important than **winning.**

Just about **anything** can be fun.

I'm thinking of all the fun I'm going to have with this piece of paper.

it's fun to use
your imagination!

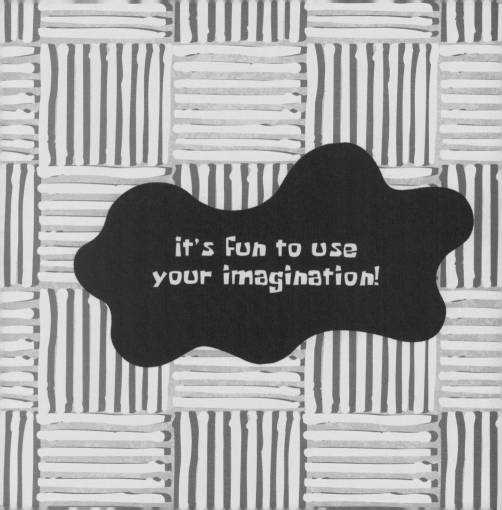

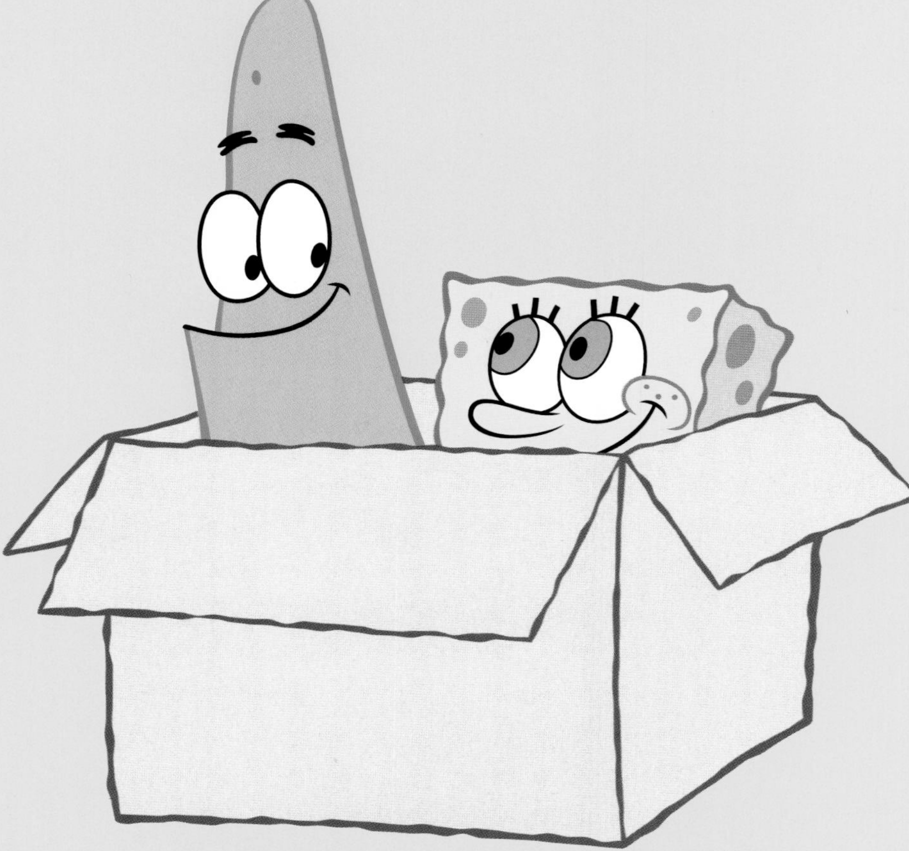

As long as you're as you're having fun, you're happy!

See how wonderful life can be
when you're MANIACAL?

Stay

positive.

People used to tell me,
"Patrick, you'll never amount to anything;
you'll always have your head in the clouds."
But just look at me now!

You don't need
everything you think
you need.

Water's For quitters!
i don't need it! i don't need it! i don't need it!

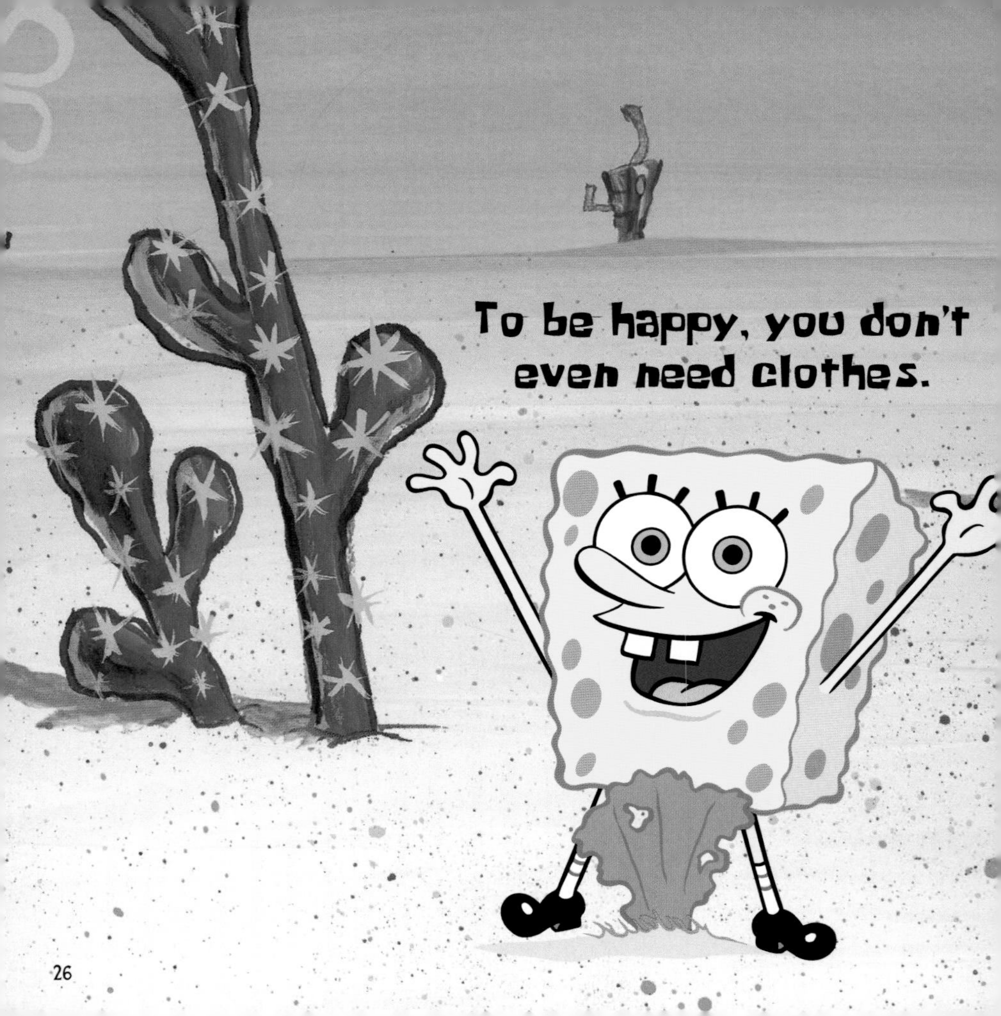

To be happy, you don't even need clothes.

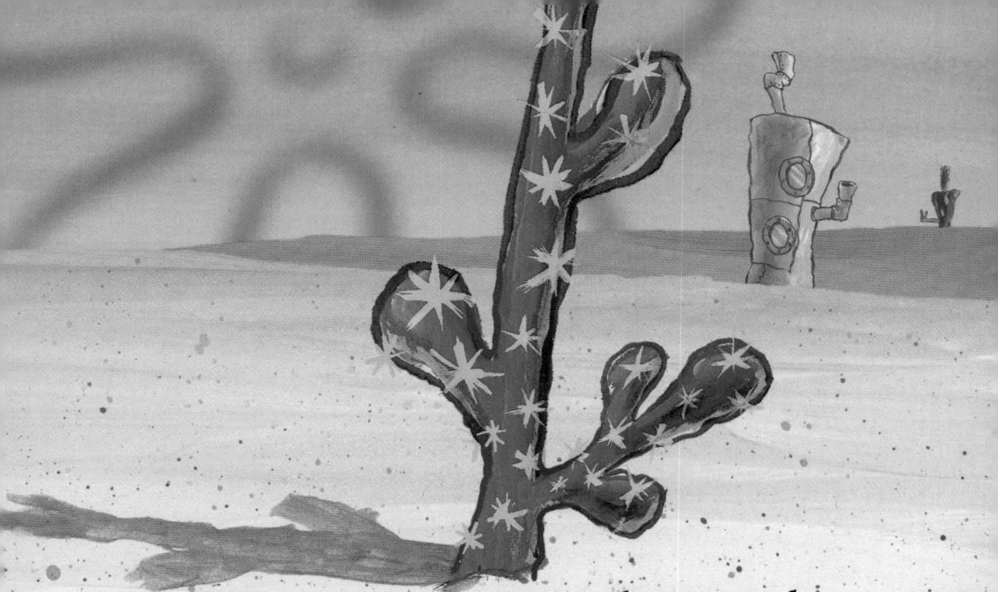

i'm going to prove that i don't need all this stuff to be happy. Maybe someday you'll wise up and join me.

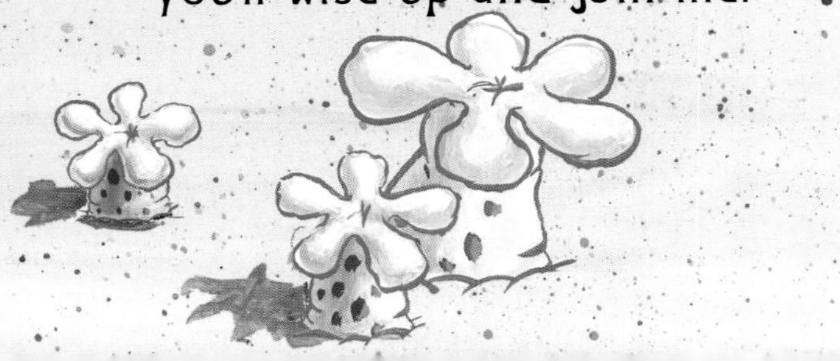

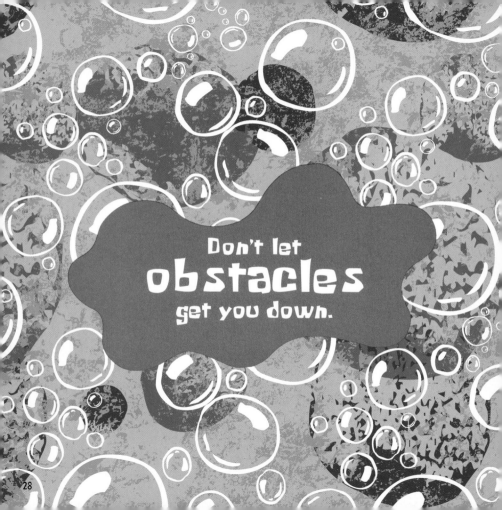

Don't let **obstacles** get you down.

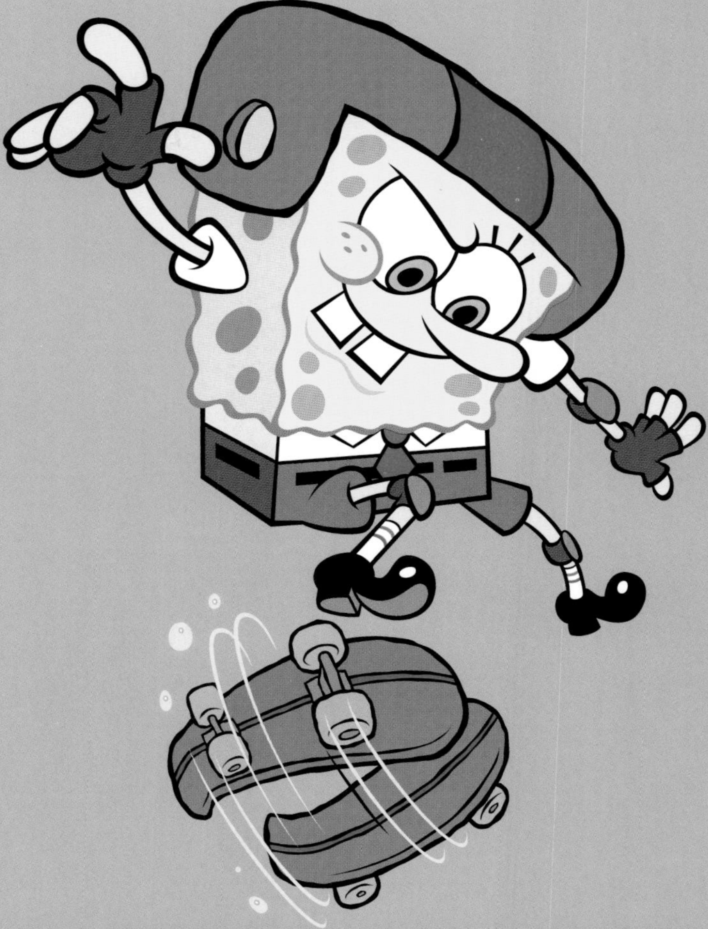

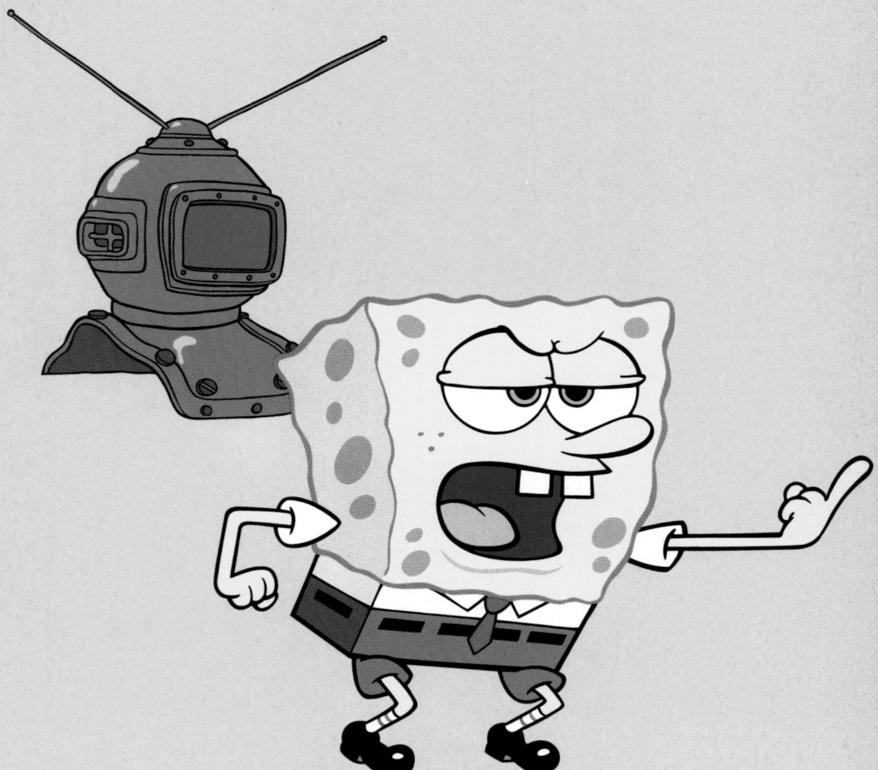

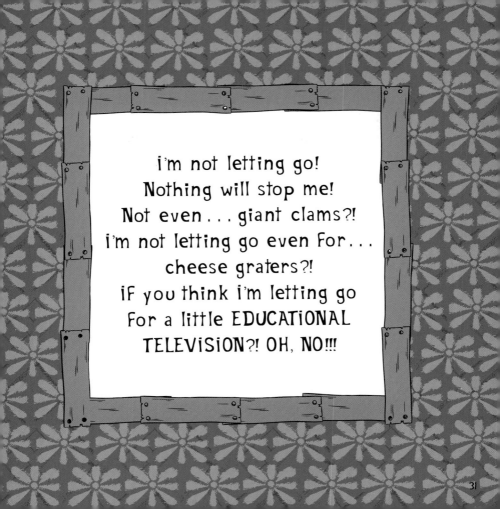

i'm not letting go!
Nothing will stop me!
Not even... giant clams?!
i'm not letting go even for...
cheese graters?!
if you think i'm letting go
for a little EDUCATIONAL
TELEVISION?! OH, NO!!!

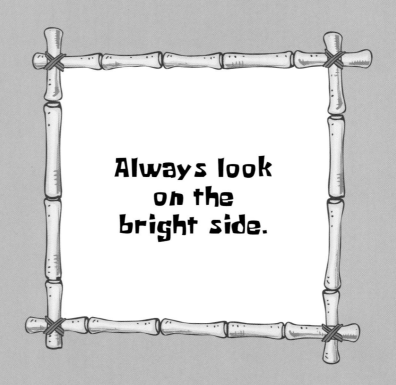

Always look
on the
bright side.

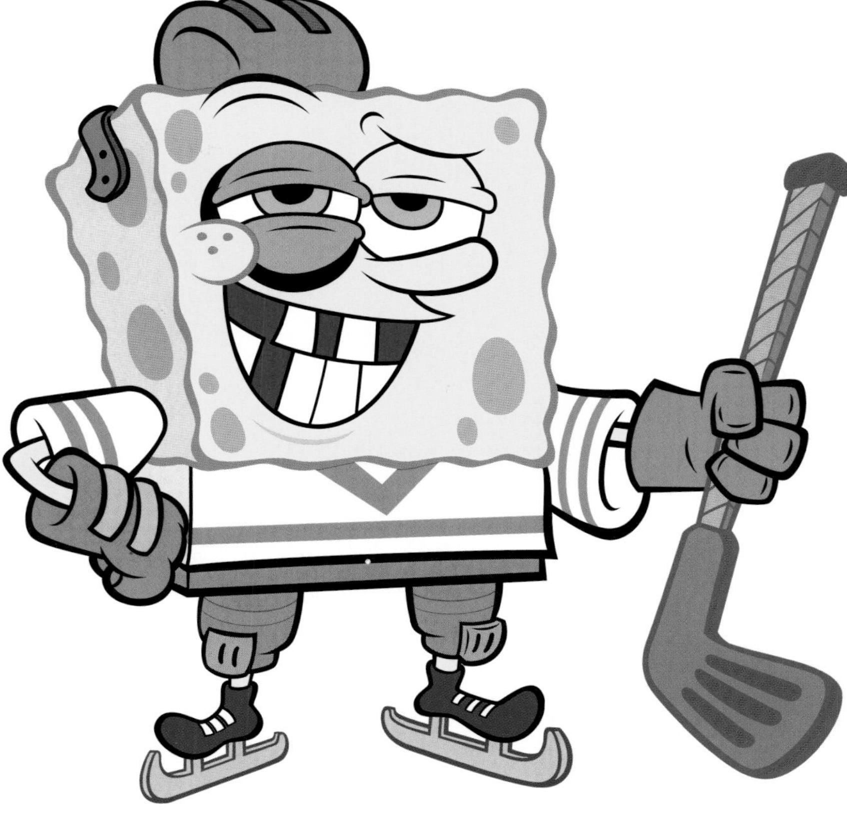

Stay **optimistic.**

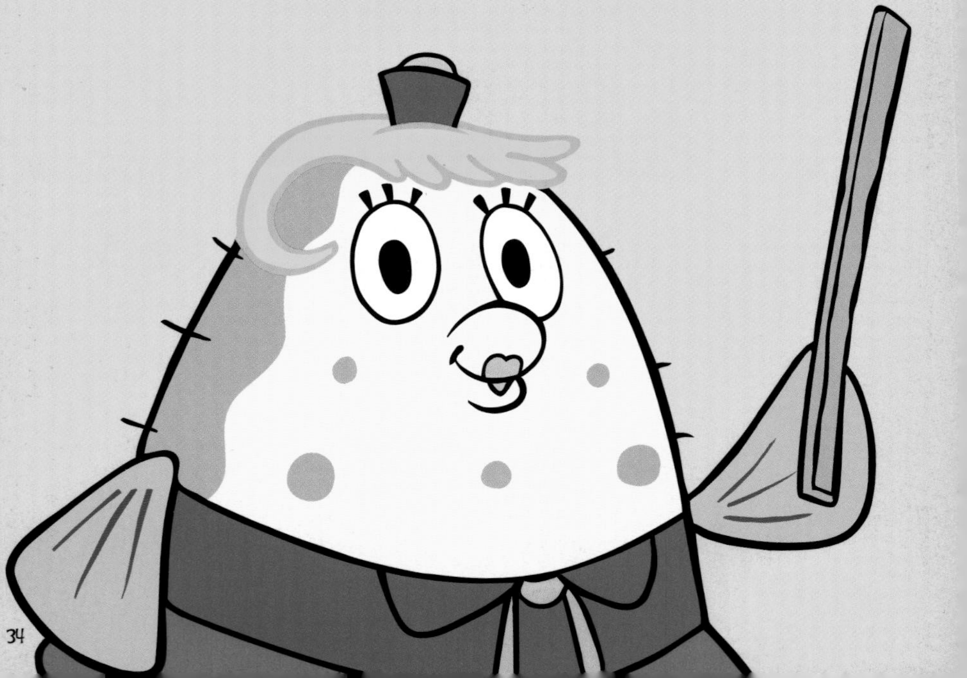

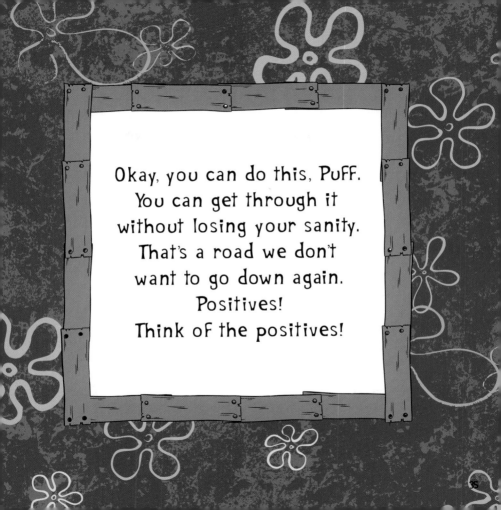

Okay, you can do this, Puff.
You can get through it
without losing your sanity.
That's a road we don't
want to go down again.
Positives!
Think of the positives!

35

Even when life seems terrible, you can find a reason to be happy!

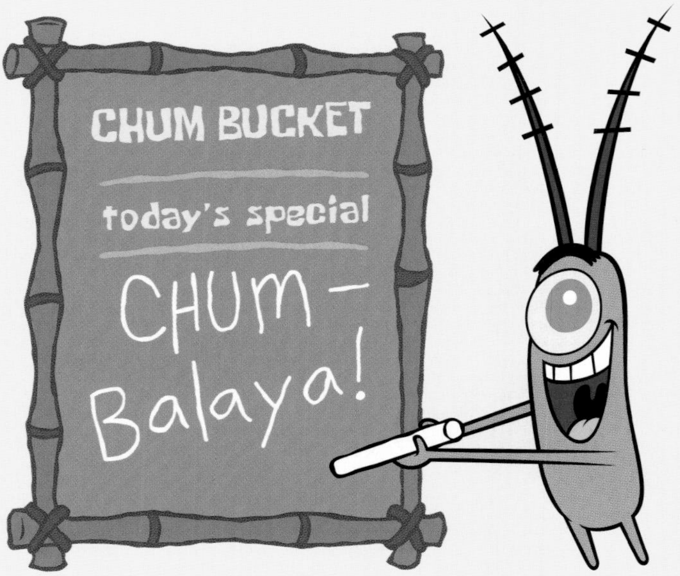
CHUM BUCKET
today's special
CHUM-
Balaya!

i may not have the Krabby Patty recipe,
but i've still got Chumbalaya!

Don't worry about little physical setbacks.

Don't worry, guys! it grows back!

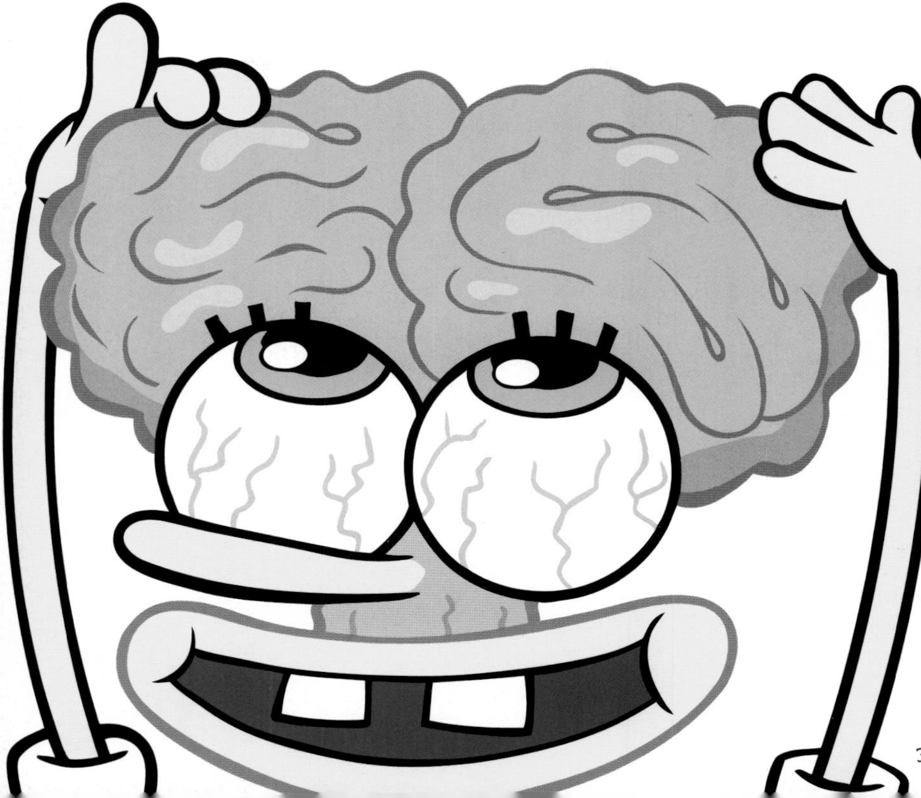

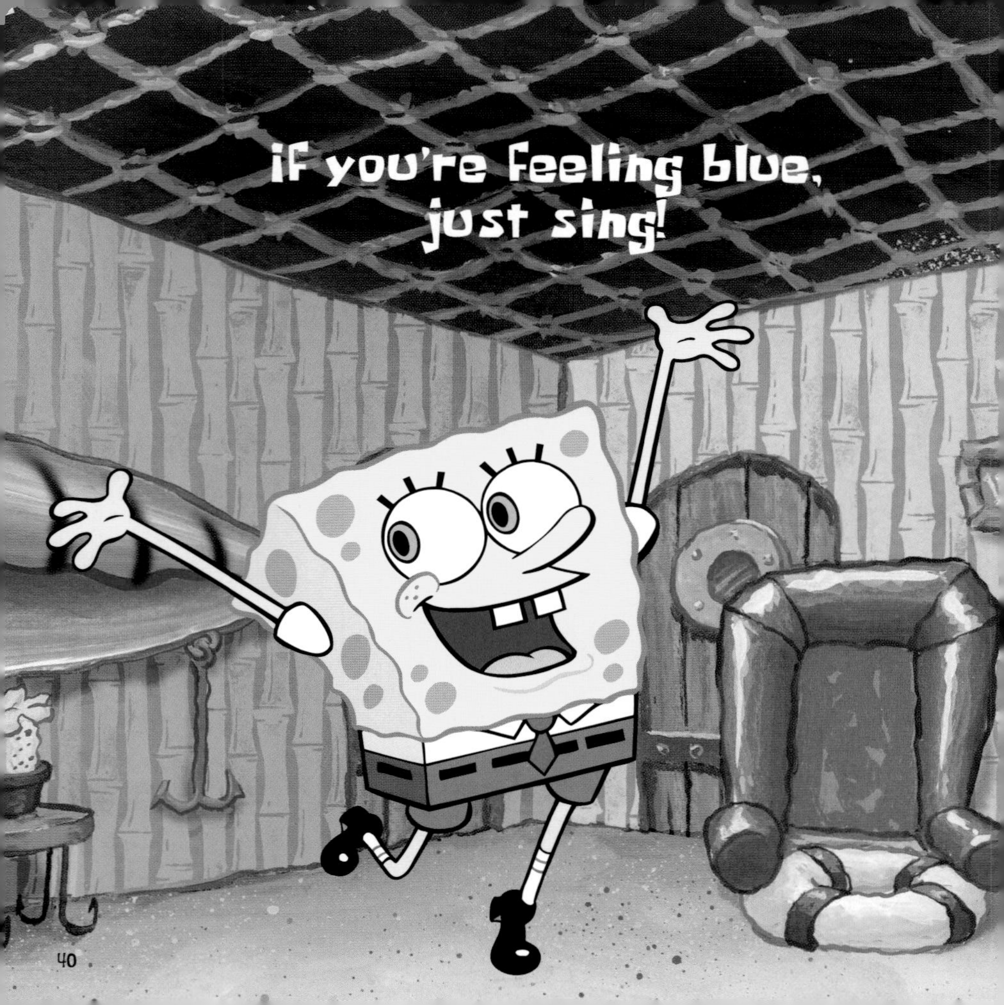

If you're feeling blue, just sing!

Let's sing our own
song about the joy
of staying indoors.
i know of a plaaaace . . .
where you never get
haaaarmed . . .
a magical plaaaace . . .
with magical chaaaarms . . .
indoors! indoors!

if you think **happy** thought.

ou'll feel happy in no time!

Oh, how touching. i'm going home to throw up.

Nothing like some **witty humor** to cheer everyone up!

Oops!
i guess i ripped my pants . . .
again.

Sometimes
being happy just
takes a little
creativity.

We've got to do something else.
Something with ... WALKIE-TALKIES!

it's hard not to
be happy
with a jellyfish.

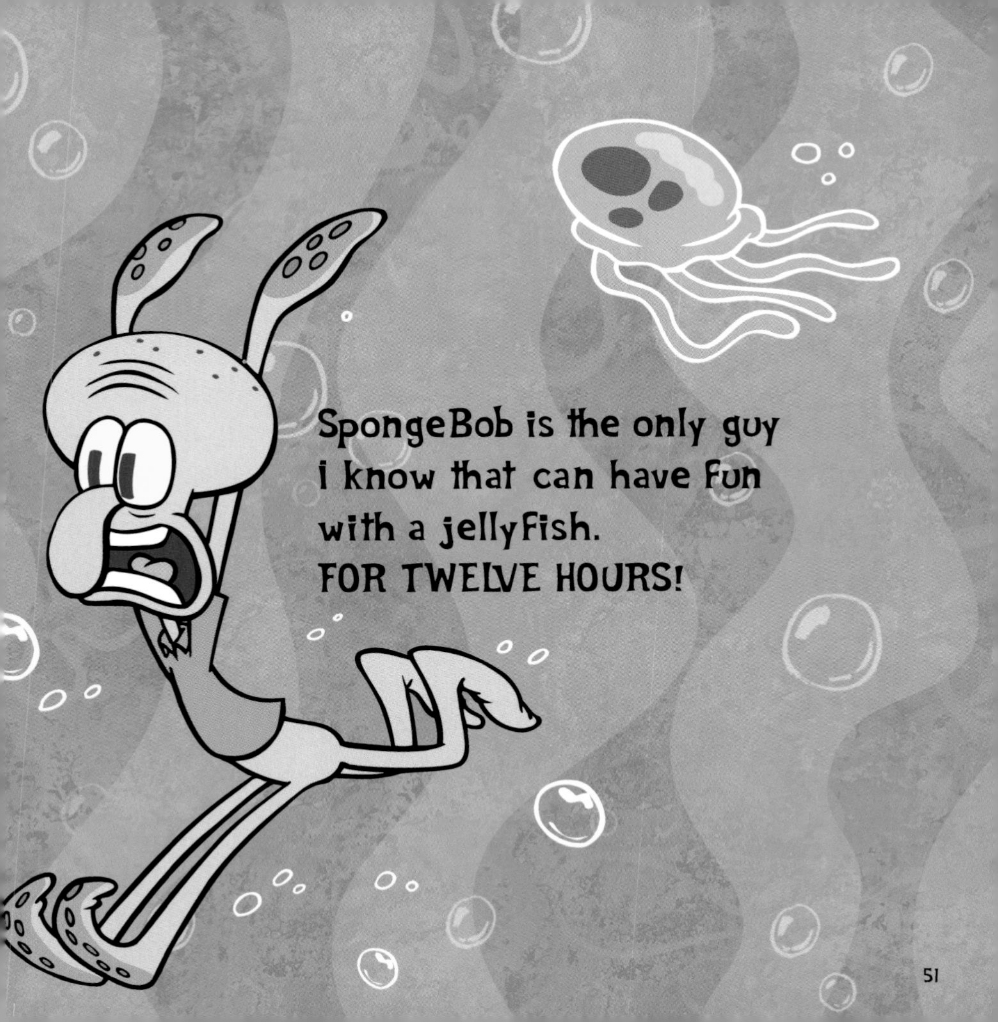

SpongeBob is the only guy
i know that can have fun
with a jellyfish.
FOR TWELVE HOURS!

Sometimes it's fun to do the

opposite

of what you normally do!

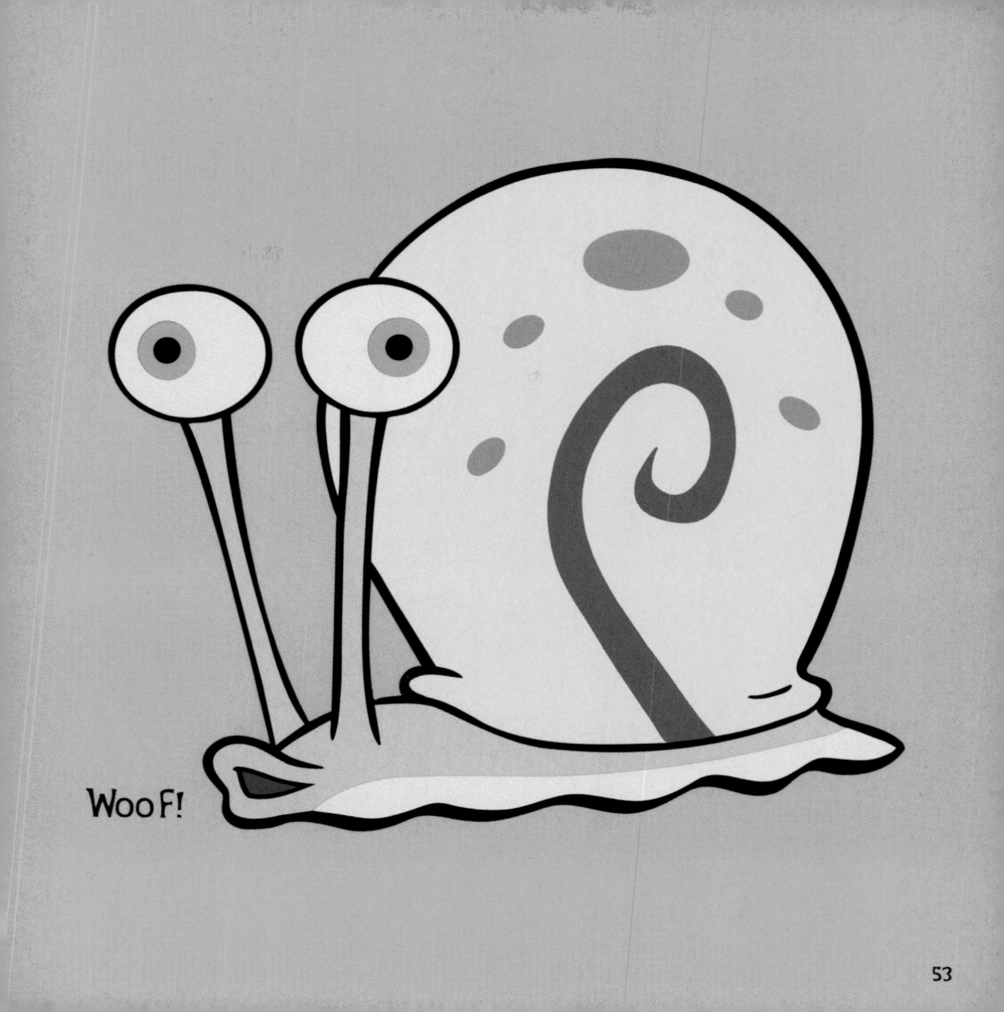

WooF!

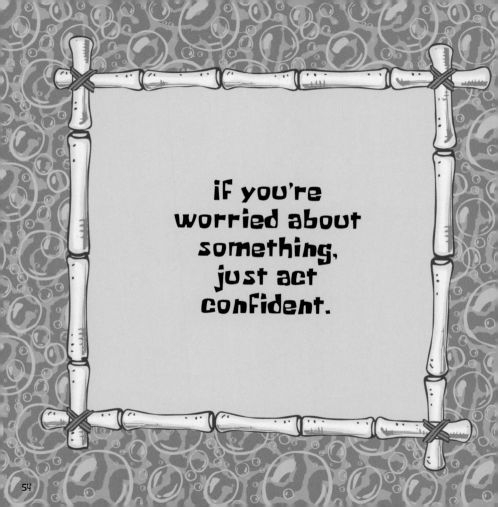

if you're worried about something, just act confident.

54

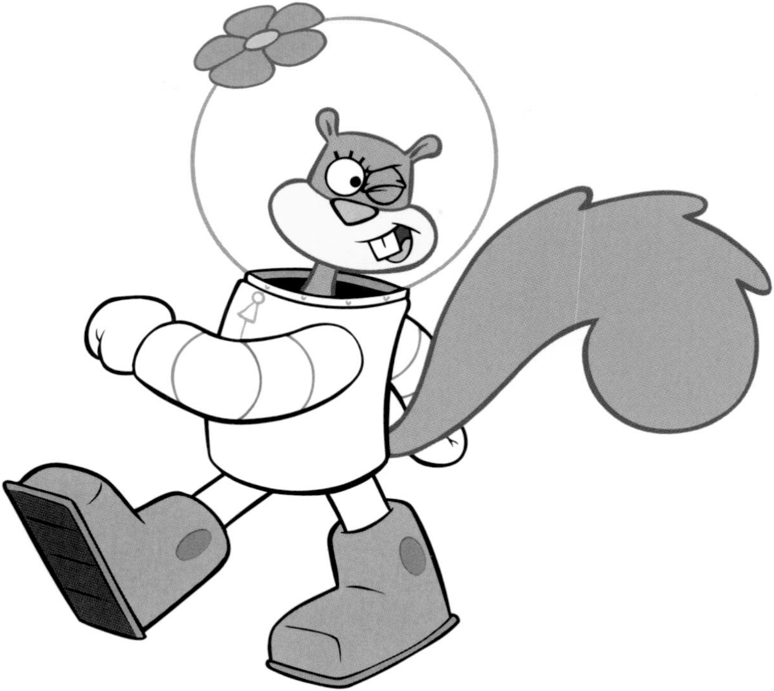

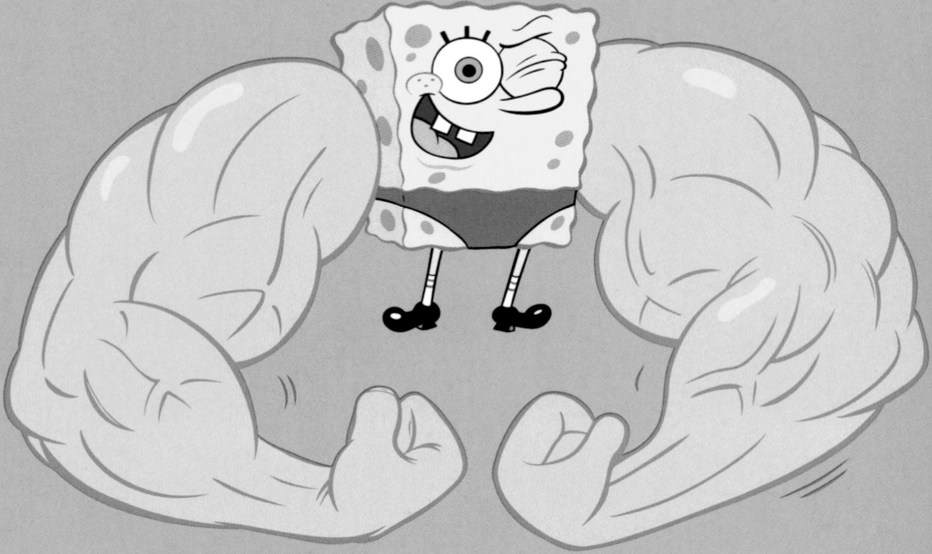

i can't give up! i've got to try! i can do it!
i've got Anchor Arms!

if you believe in yourself, you'll be happy.

A happy face can make a happy heart!

After all these years,
i thought i was the
master of torture.
But THAT —
that just wasn't FAIR!

Anyone can be happy,
as long as they
never give up!

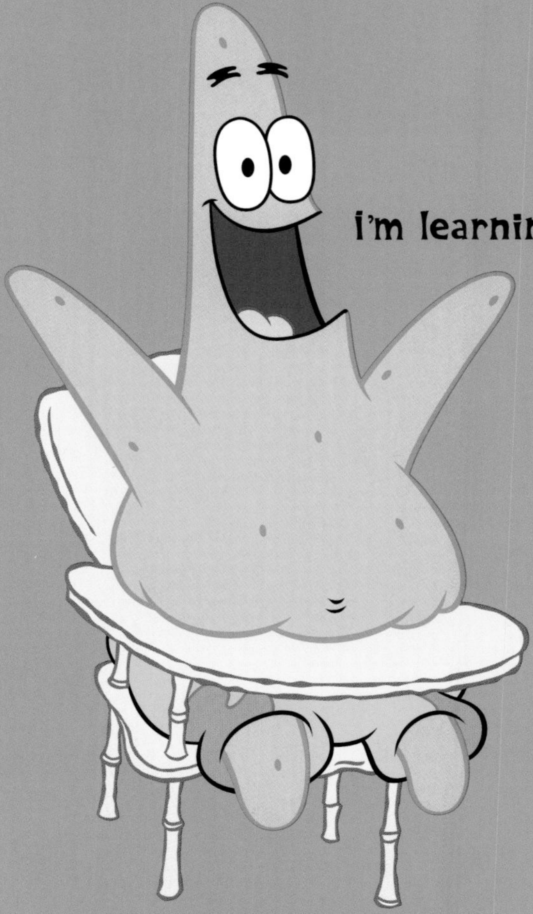

I'm learning!

One good way to get
happy is to get naked!

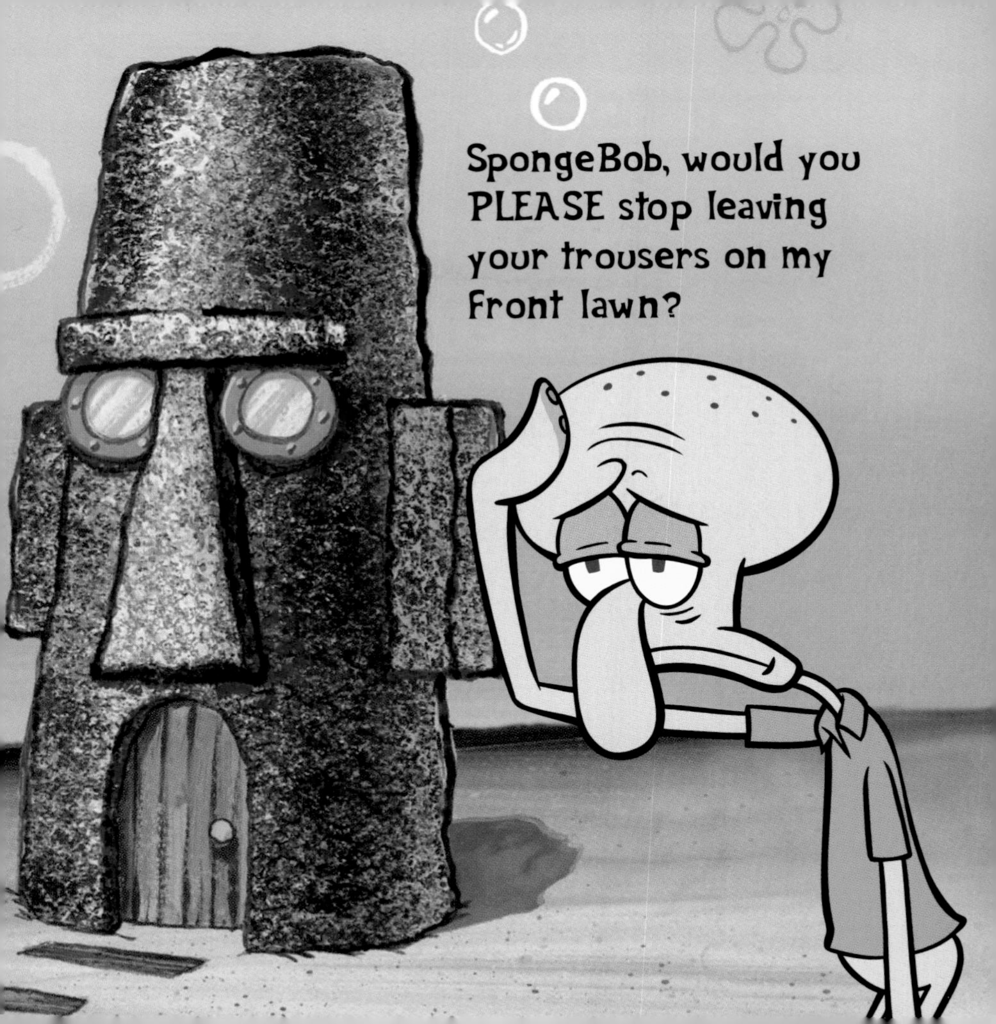
SpongeBob, would you PLEASE stop leaving your trousers on my front lawn?

You can
be happy and
still act
like an adult.

Allow me to demonstrate. First, puff out your chest. Now say "tax exemption."

Sometimes you just
have to cut loose!

Life's as extreme as you wanna make it!

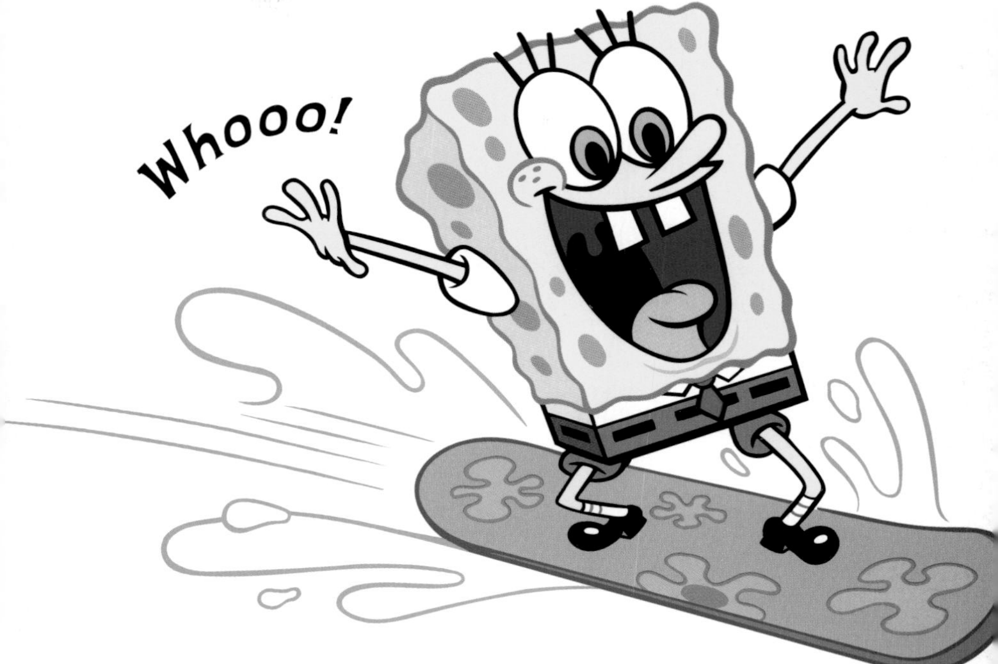
Whooo!

Devote plenty of time to your hobbies.

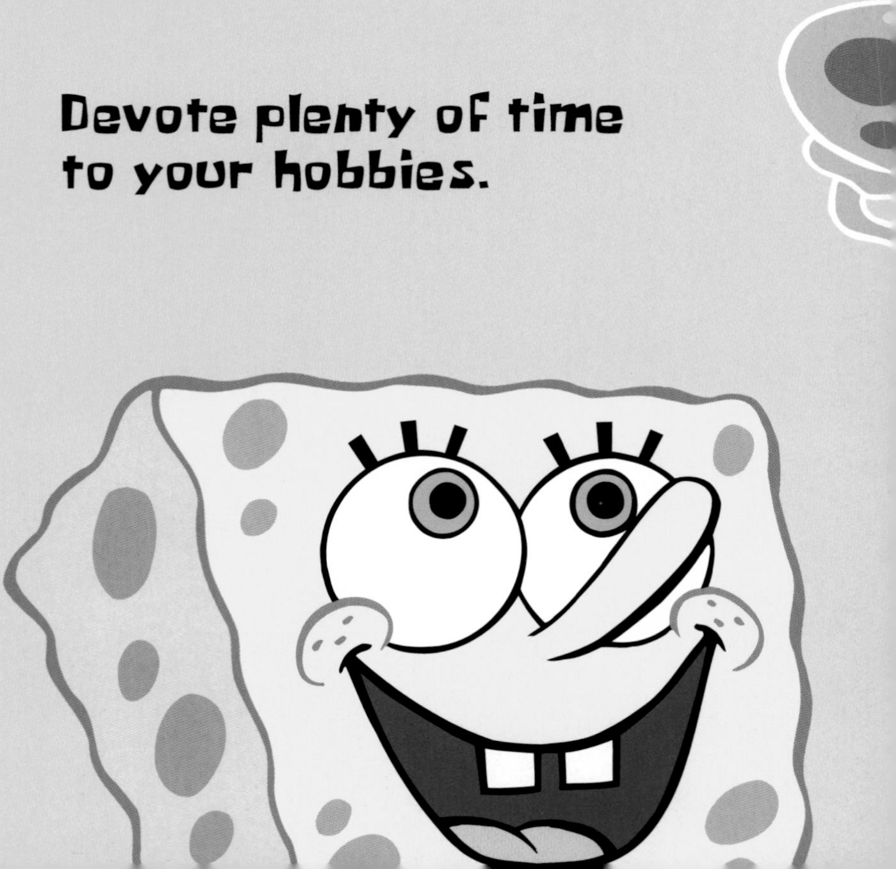

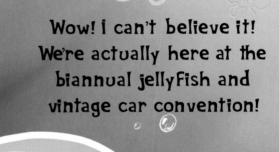

Wow! I can't believe it! We're actually here at the biannual jellyfish and vintage car convention!

Blowing bubbles
is a great way
to get happy!

As much as i love cruel, sick jokes,
i'm afraid he's not joking.

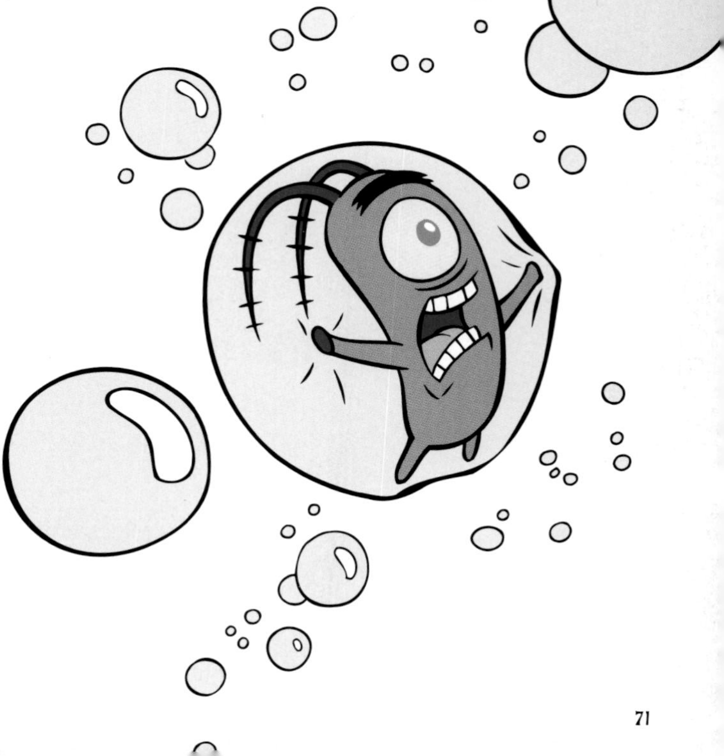

Everybody
has something
that makes them
really happy.

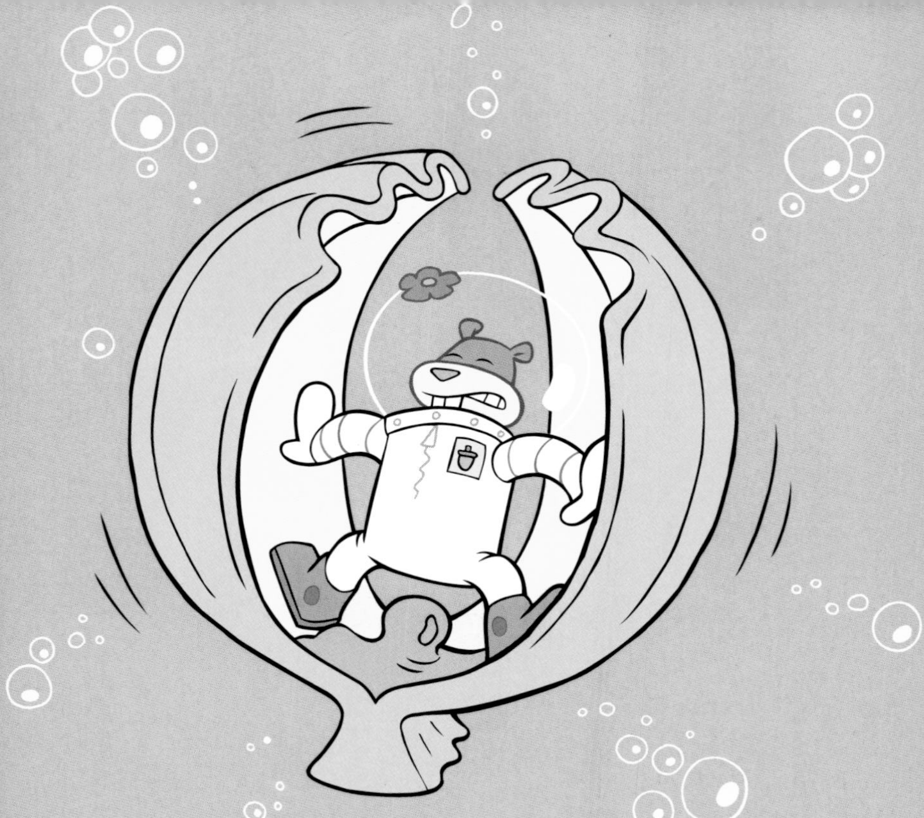

Clam wrestling!

it can make
you happy
just to see
someone
else being
happy.

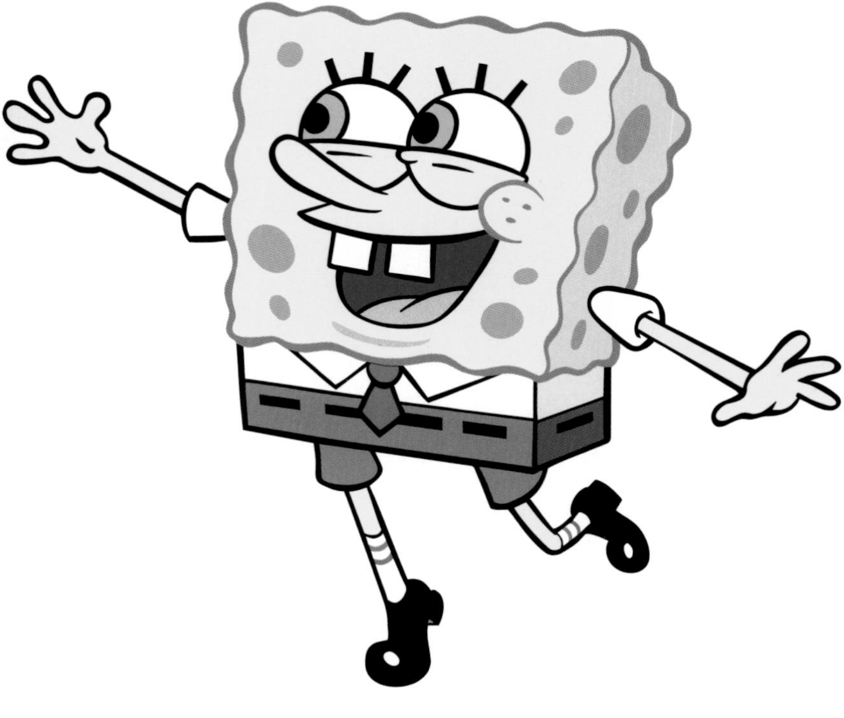

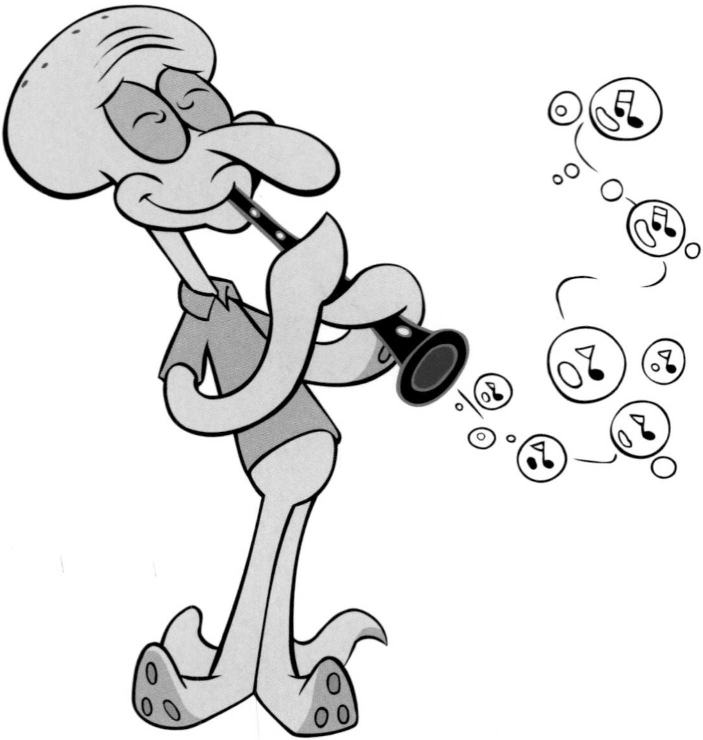

That was great, Squidward! All those wrong notes you play make it sound more original!

Feeling happy is like having Grandma's **yummy** cookies in your tummy.

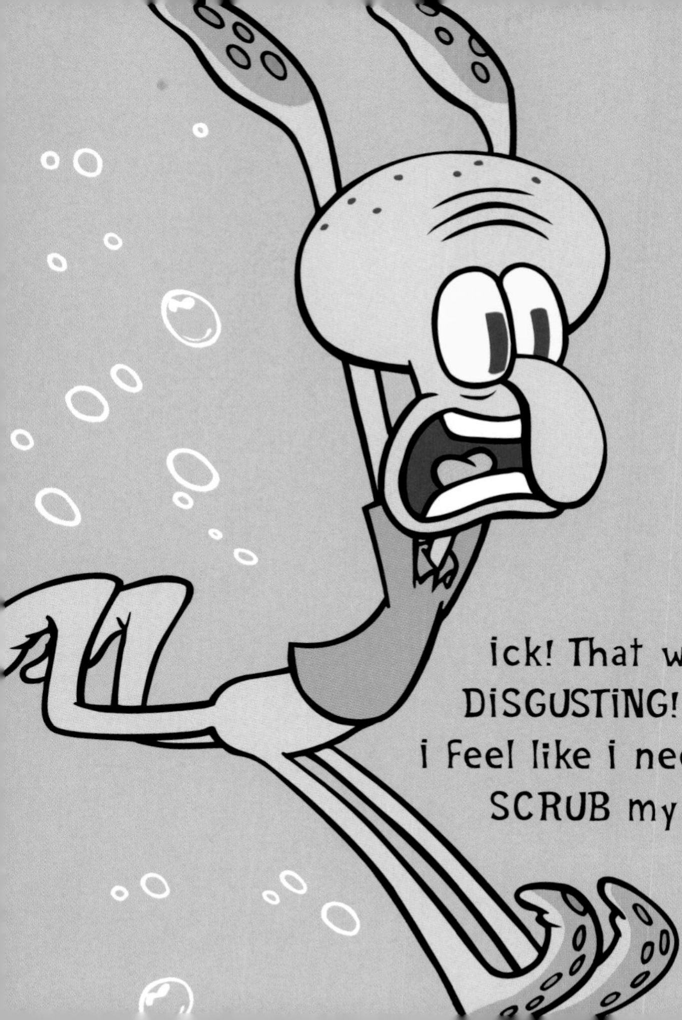

ick! That was
DISGUSTING!
i Feel like i need to
SCRUB myself!

A simple change
in the weather
can make you happy.

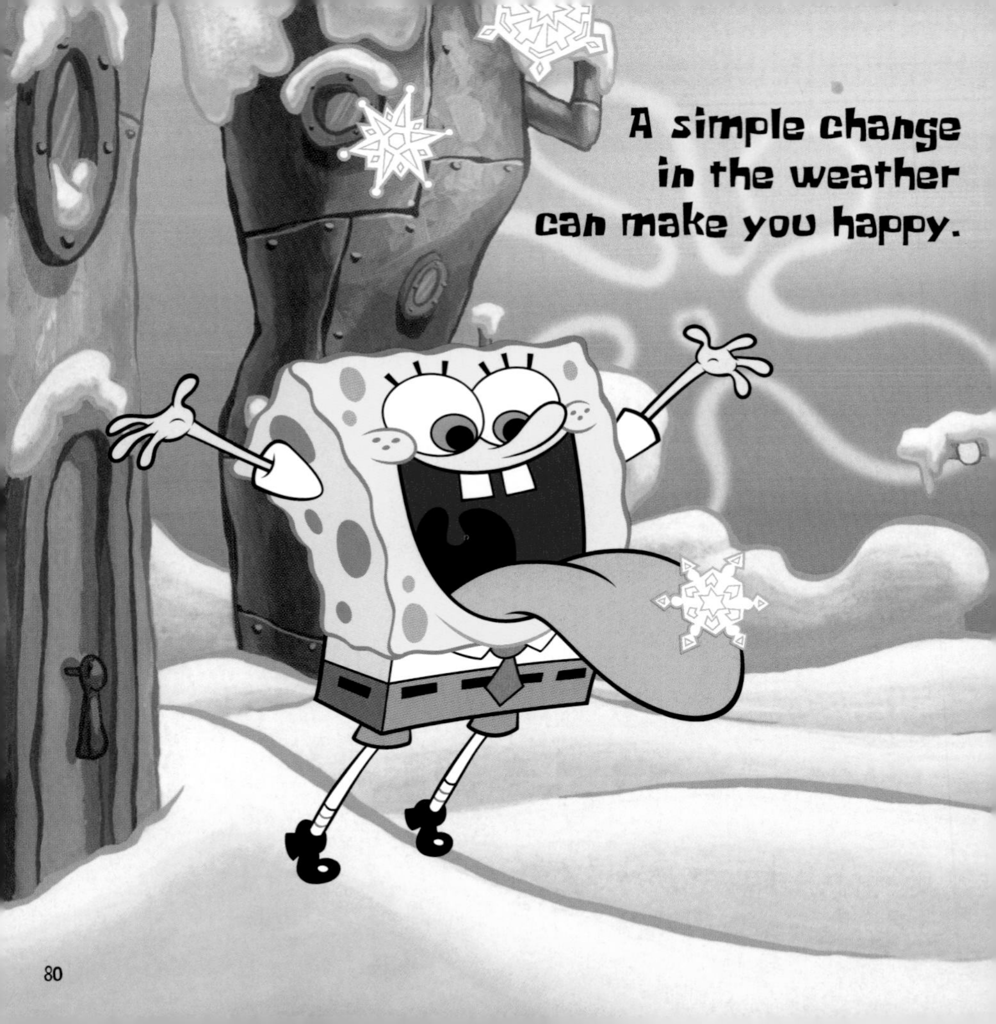

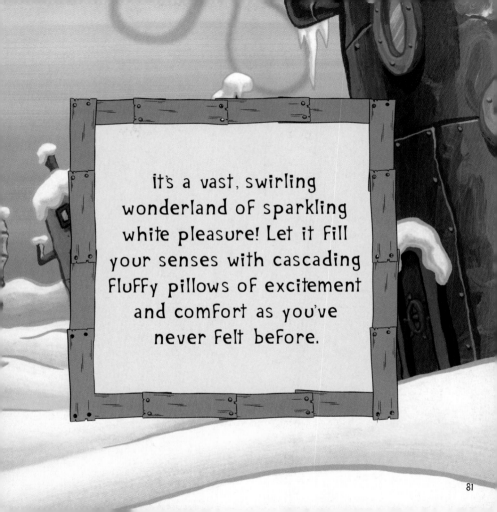

it's a vast, swirling wonderland of sparkling white pleasure! Let it fill your senses with cascading fluffy pillows of excitement and comfort as you've never felt before.

Remember, money can't
make you happy.

Are you on some
new allergy
medication, boy?!

in the end, your happiness is the most important thing.

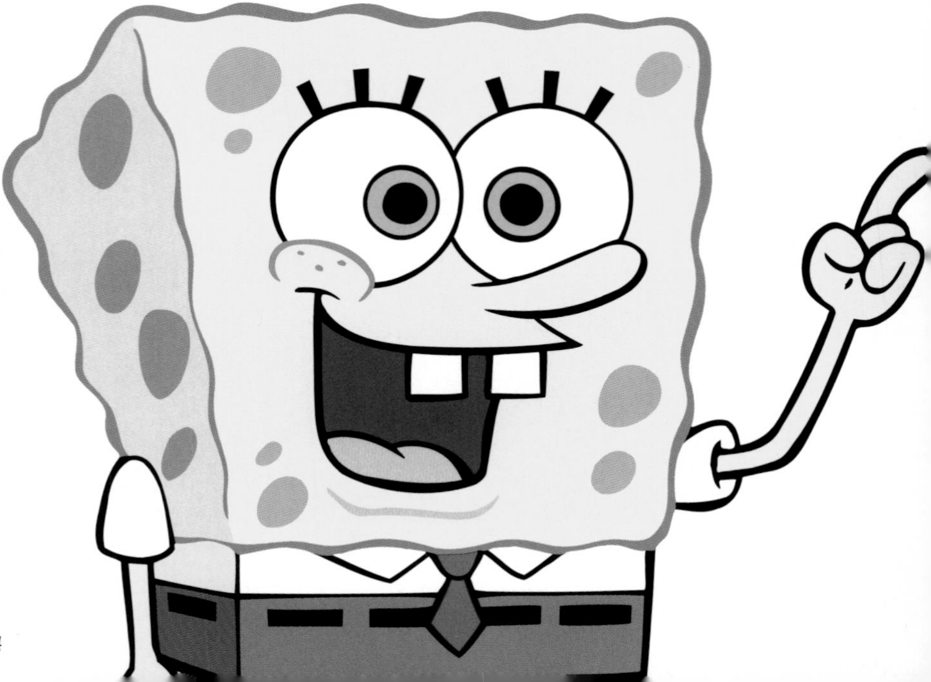

You know, if I were
to die right now in some sort
of fiery explosion
due to the carelessness
of a friend . . .
well, that'd be just okay.

85

At the end of a happy day, i like to happily soak in my happy tub.

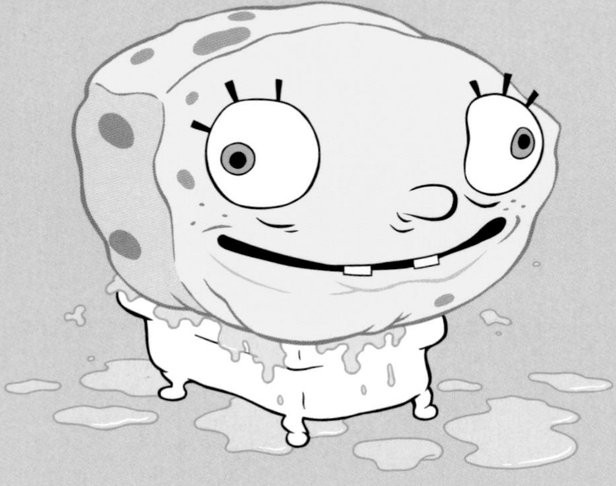

Well, that was more of SpongeBob than i needed to see.

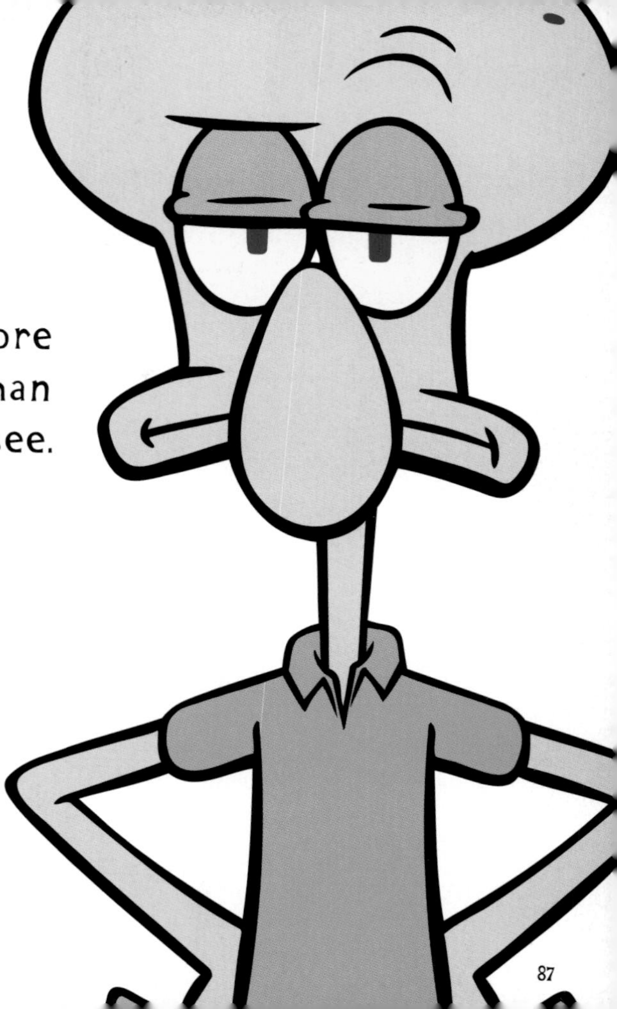

A little snack will give you happy dreams.

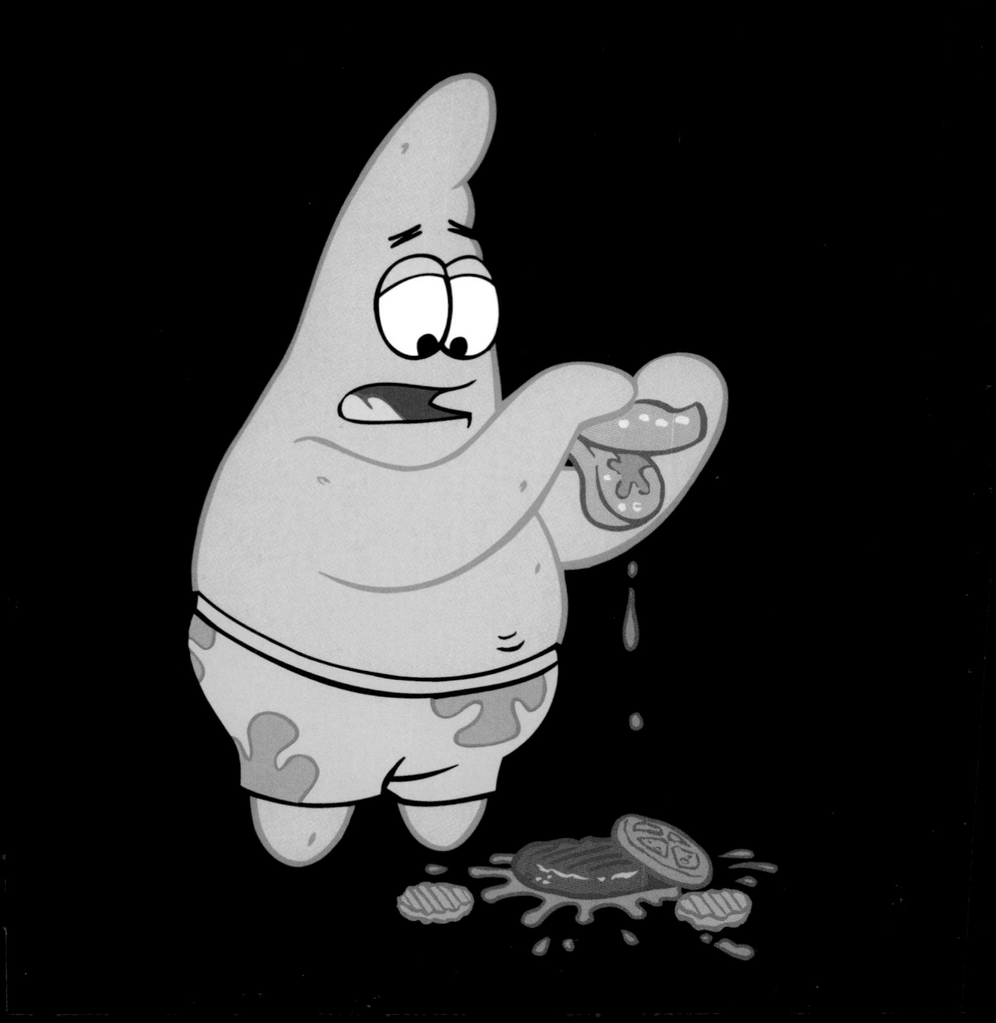

Tomorrow will be another happy day!

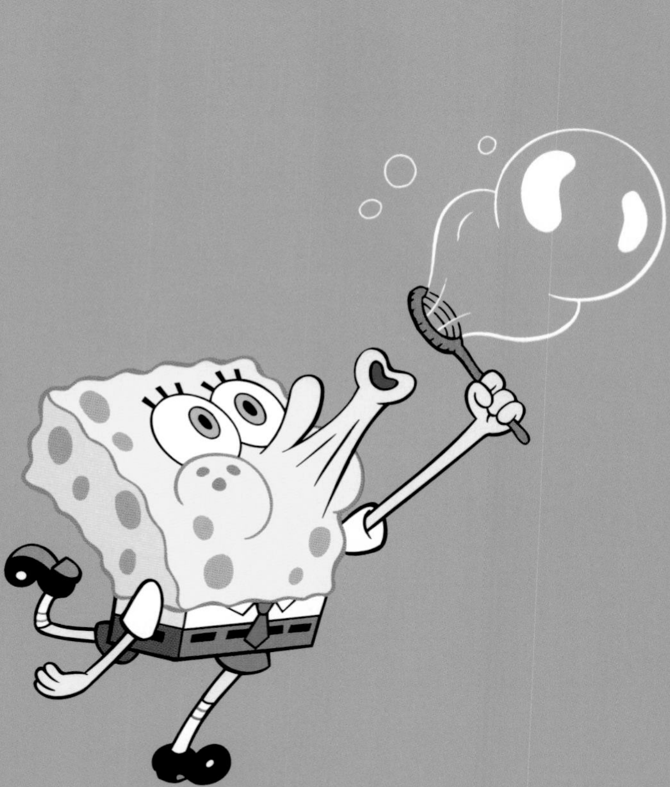

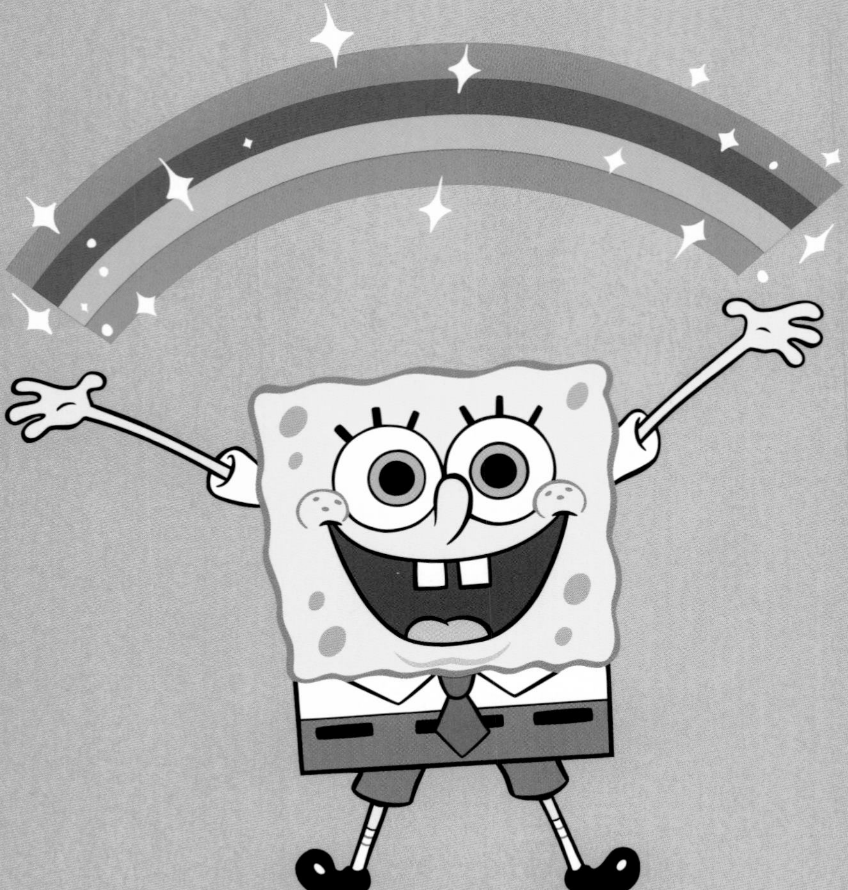

And with a tiny pinch of magic AAAALL your dreams can come true!

Happy, happy, happy

happy, happy, happy!

Well, that's it. I'm getting off the loony express.

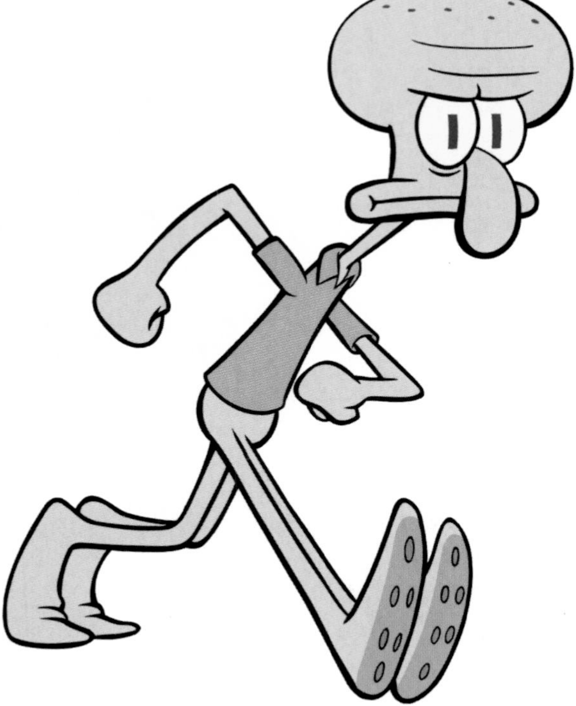